MY FIRST EASY COLOURING BOOK

MOONSTONE

Published in Moonstone
by Rupa Publications India Pvt. Ltd 2024
7/16, Ansari Road, Daryaganj
New Delhi 110002

Sales centres:
Bengaluru Chennai
Hyderabad Jaipur Kathmandu
Kolkata Mumbai Prayagraj

Copyright © Rupa Publications India Pvt. Ltd 2024

All rights reserved.
No part of this publication may be reproduced, transmitted,
or stored in a retrieval system, in any form or by any means,
electronic, mechanical, photocopying, recording or otherwise,
without the prior permission of the publisher.

P-ISBN: 978-93-6156-734-6

First impression 2024

10 9 8 7 6 5 4 3 2 1

Printed in India
This book is sold subject to the condition that it shall not,
by way of trade or otherwise, be lent, resold, hired out, or otherwise
circulated, without the publisher's prior consent, in any form of binding
or cover other than that in which it is published.

Bb

Bat

Cc

Cat

Dd

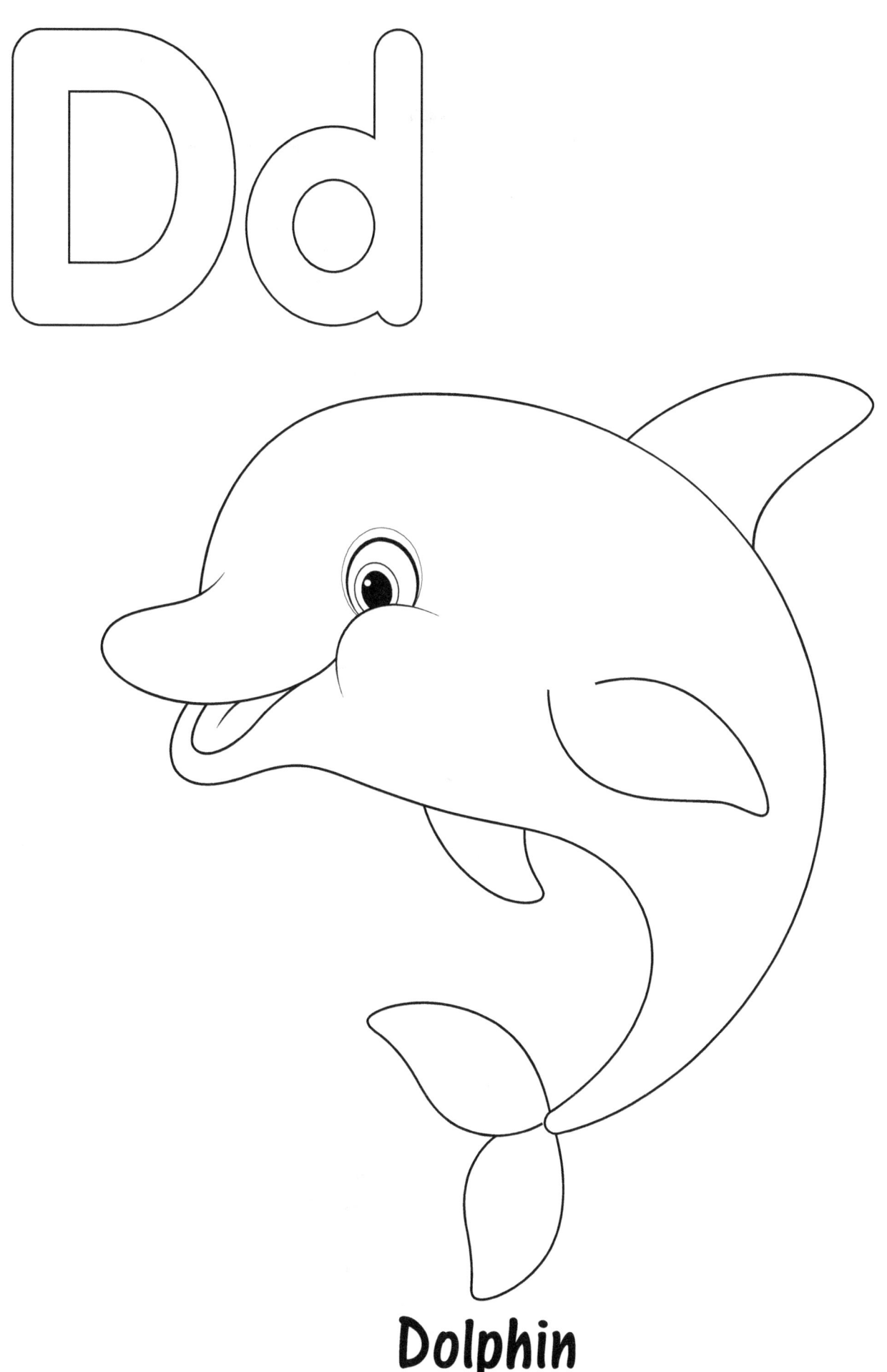

Dolphin

Ee

Elephant

Ff

Frog

Hh

Hat

Ii

Ice cream

Kk

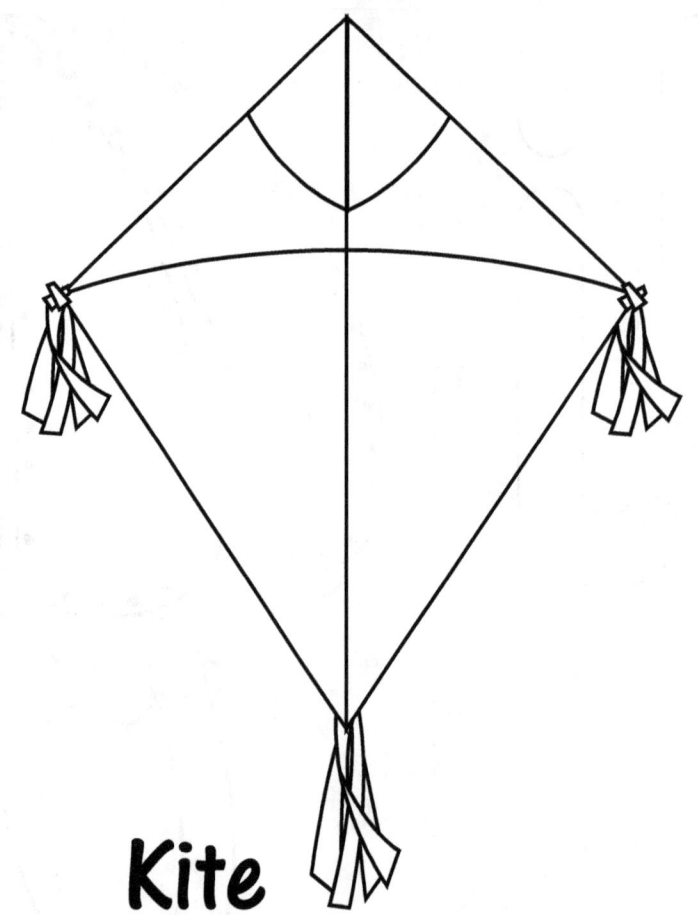

Kite

Ll

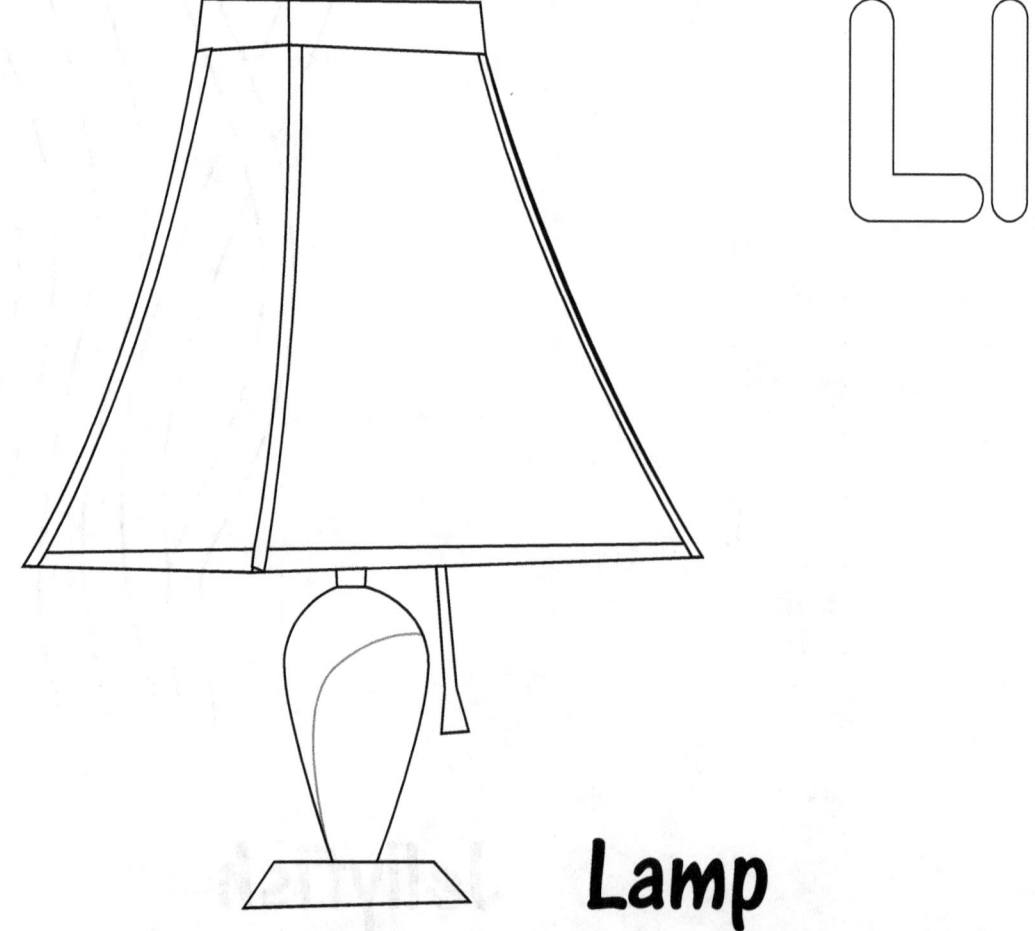

Lamp

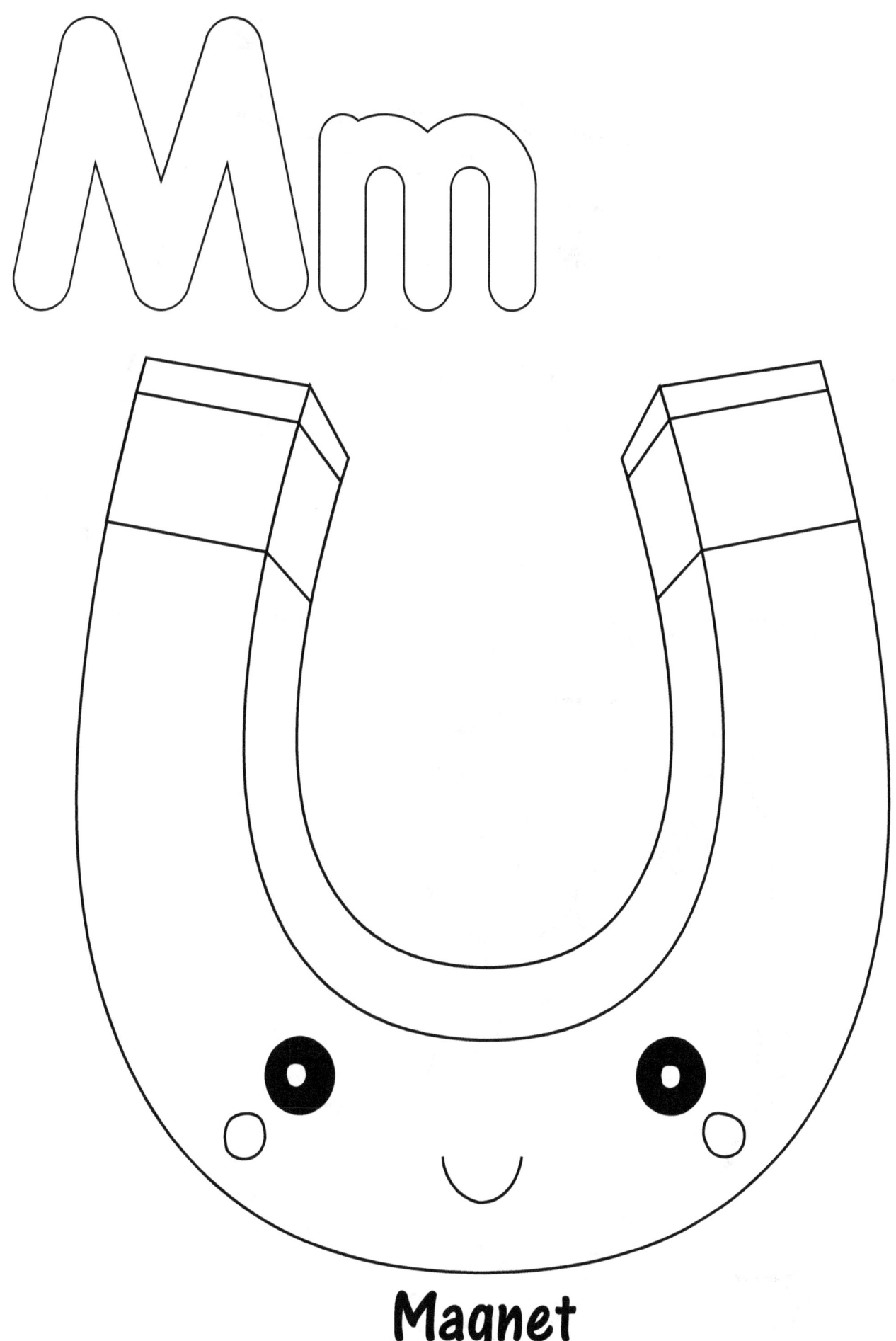

Magnet

Nn

Notebook

Oo

Owl

Qq

Queen

Rr

Rainbow

Ss

Sun

Tt

Tomato

Uu

Umbrella

Vv

Volcano

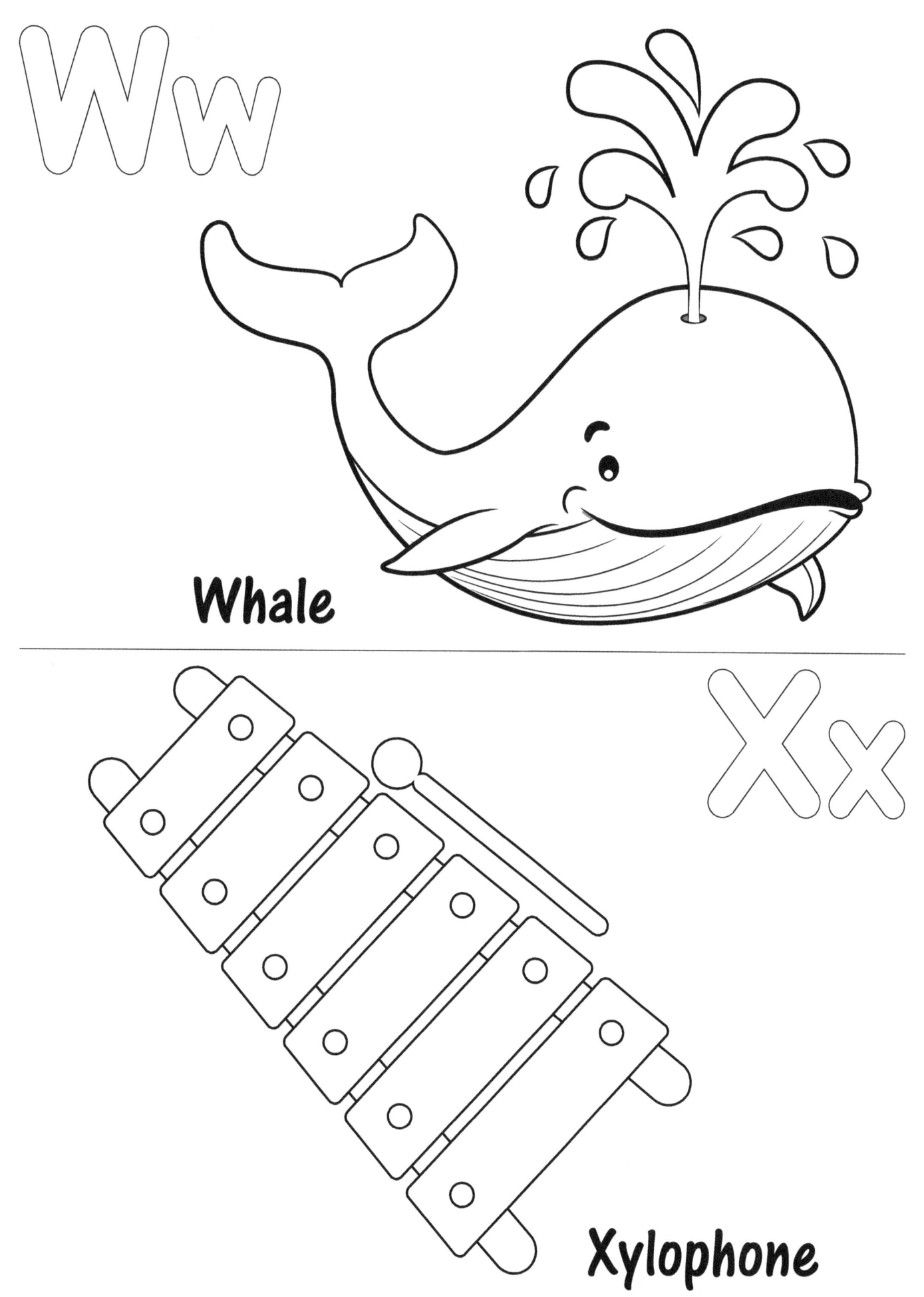

Yy

Yo-yo

Zz

Zebra

CUTE ANIMALS

Fox

Dog

Monkey

Rhinoceros

Cow

Goat

Deer

Pig

Donkey

Bear

Squirrel

Tiger

Lion

Crocodile

Elephant

Chick

Apple

Tomato

Mango

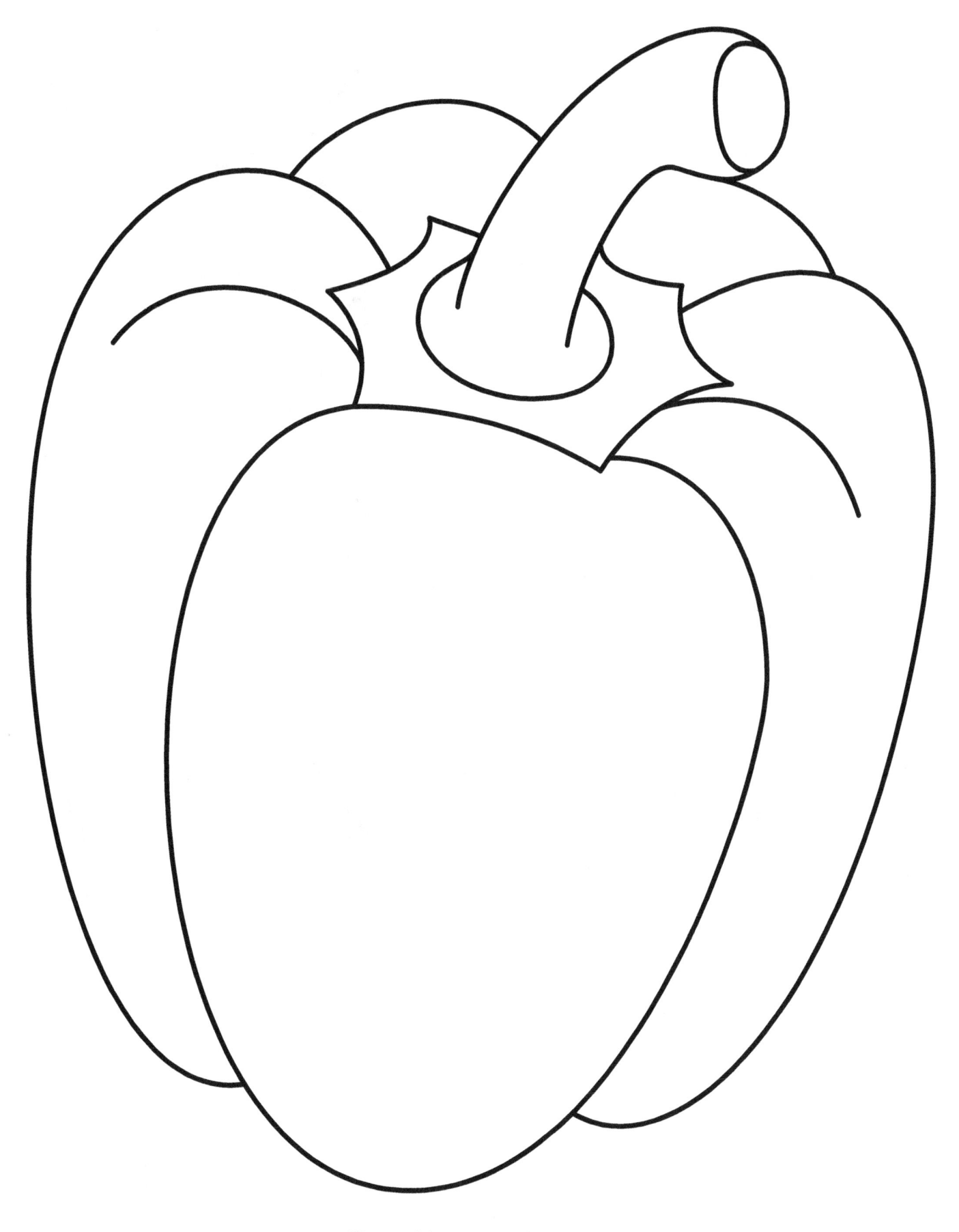

Bell pepper

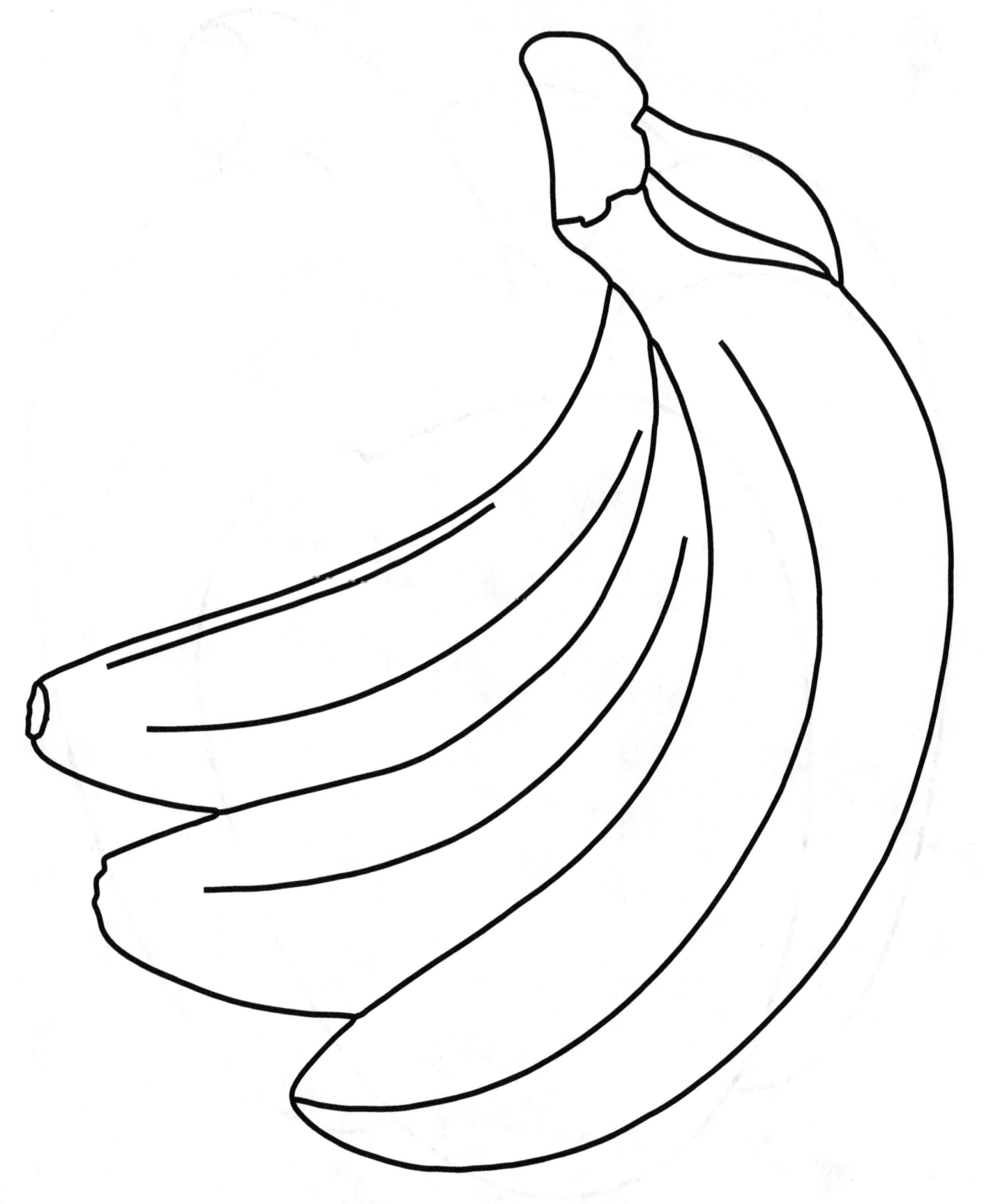
Banana

Pumpkin

Grapes

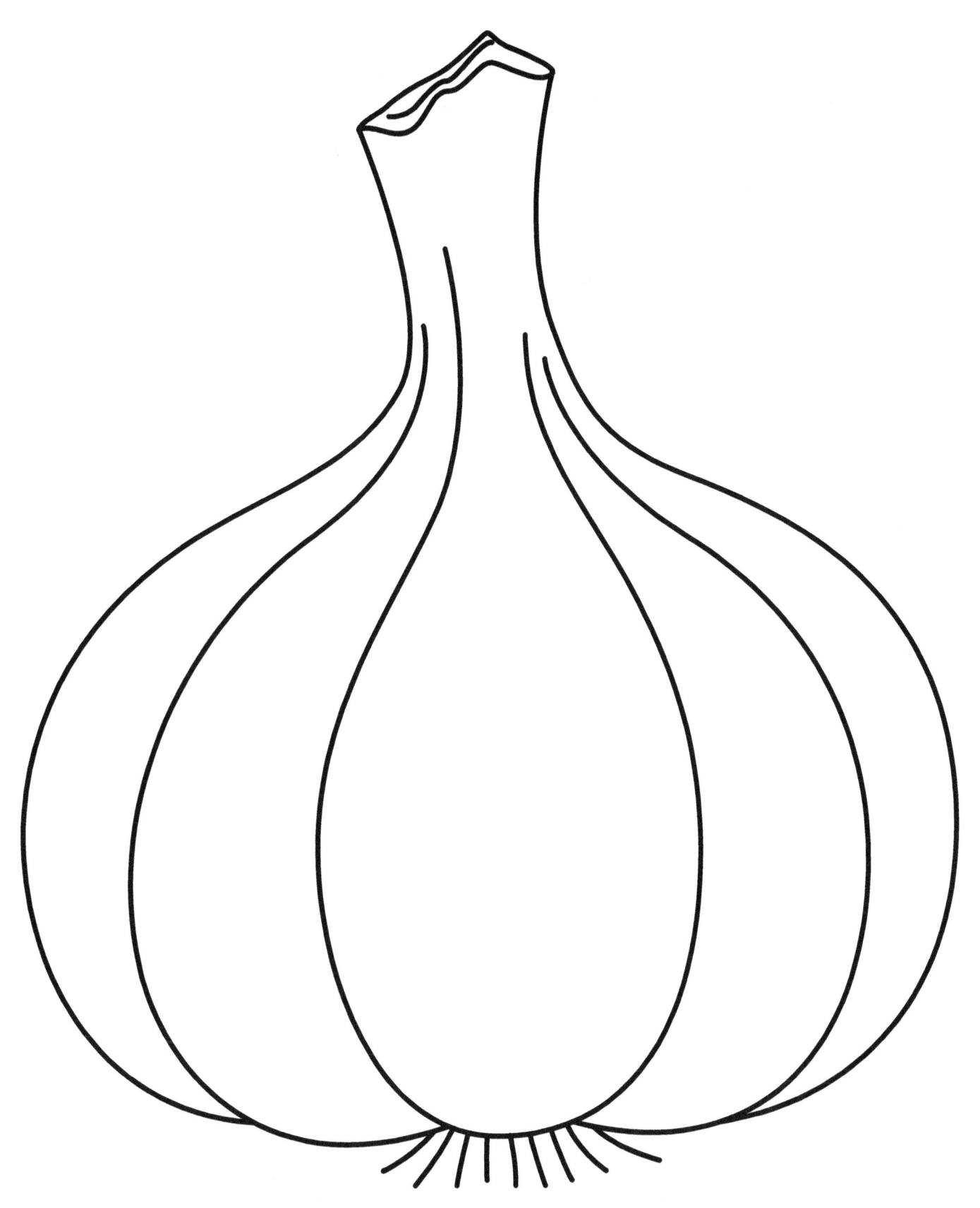

Cauliflower

Strawberry

Eggplant

Watermelon

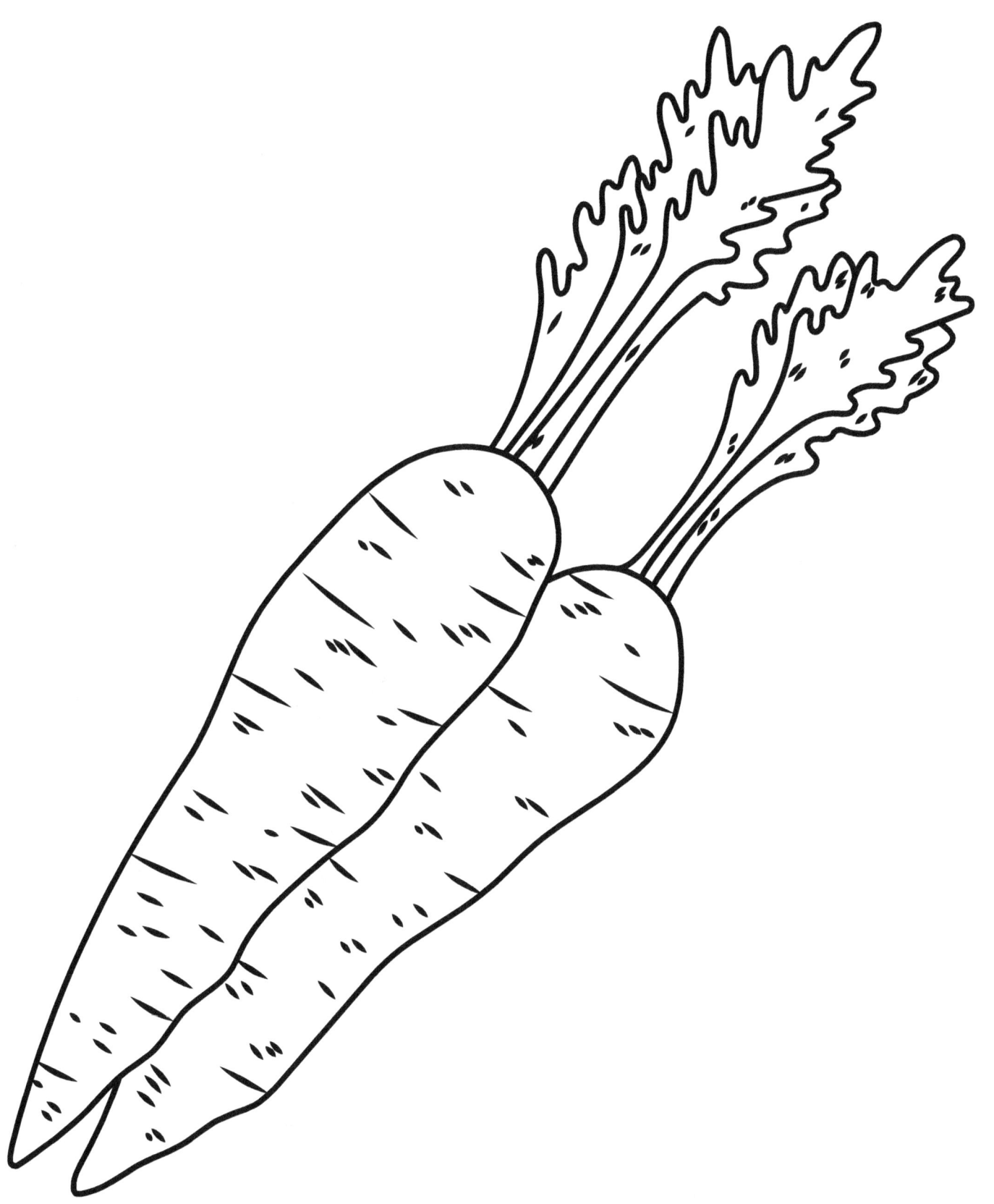

Carrot

Kiwi

Car

Bicycle

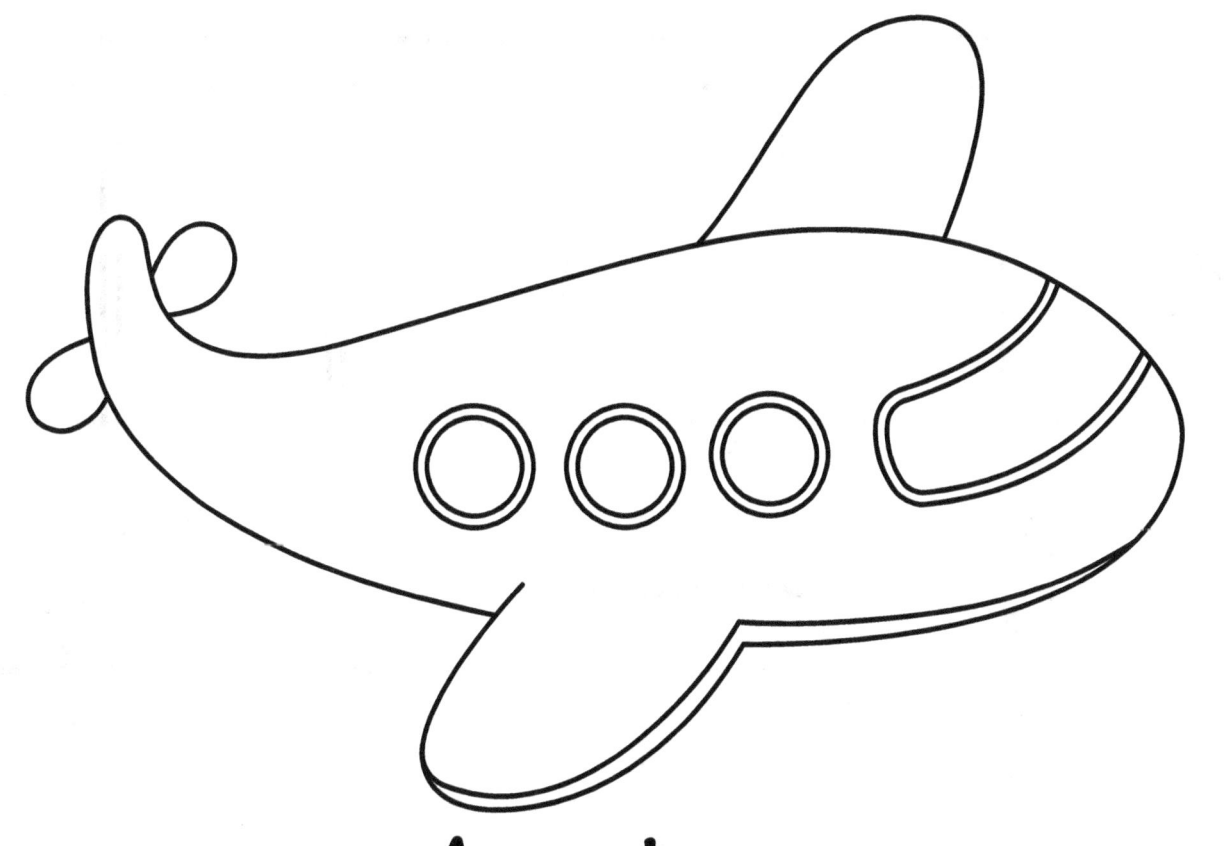

Crane

Aeroplane

Ship

Bus

Pickup Truck

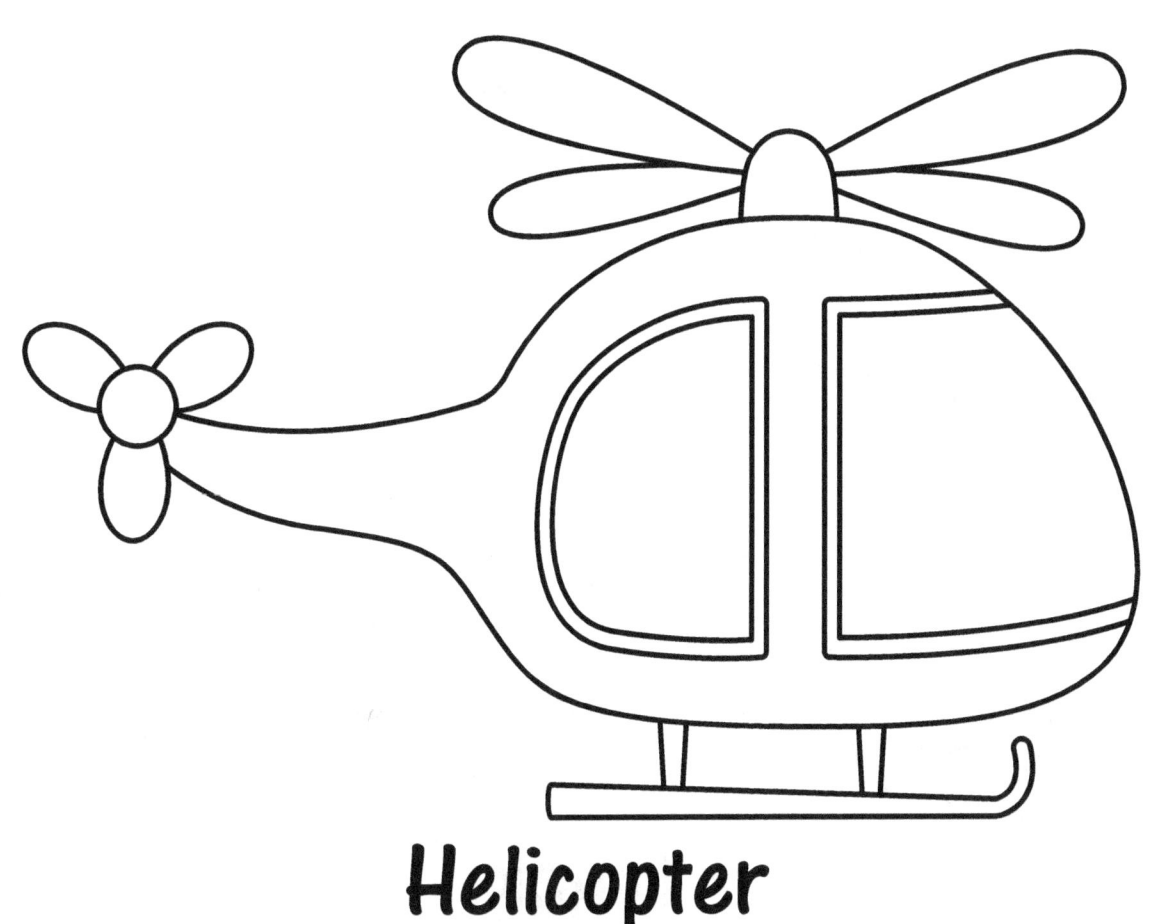

Helicopter

Police Car

Truck

Wagon

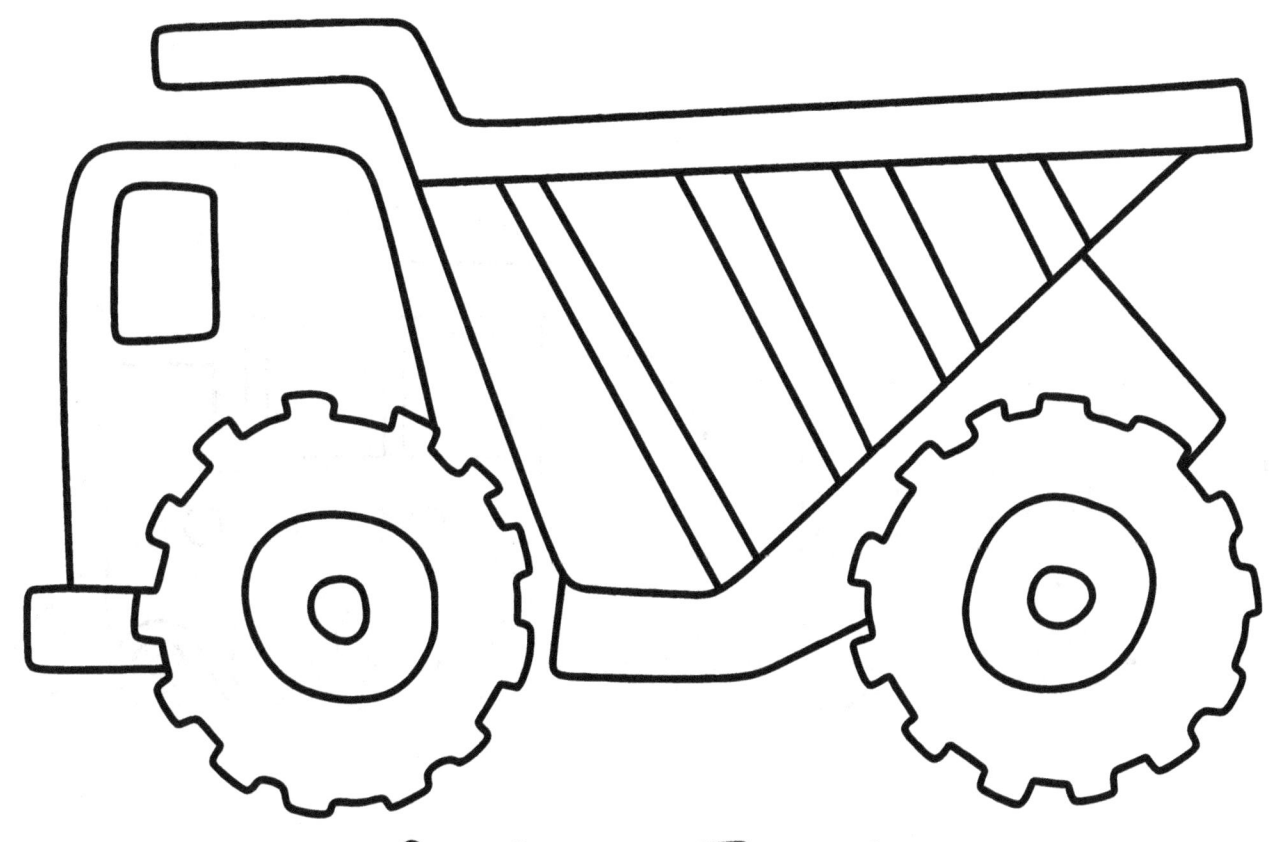

Garbage Truck

Excavator Machine

Train

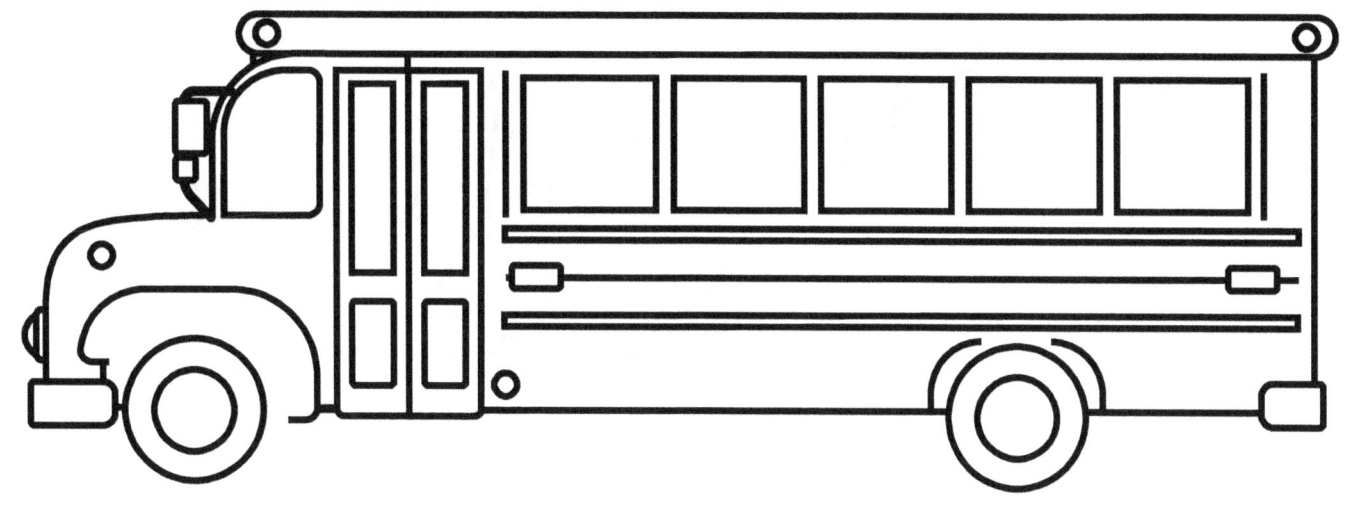

School Bus

Monster Truck

Mixer

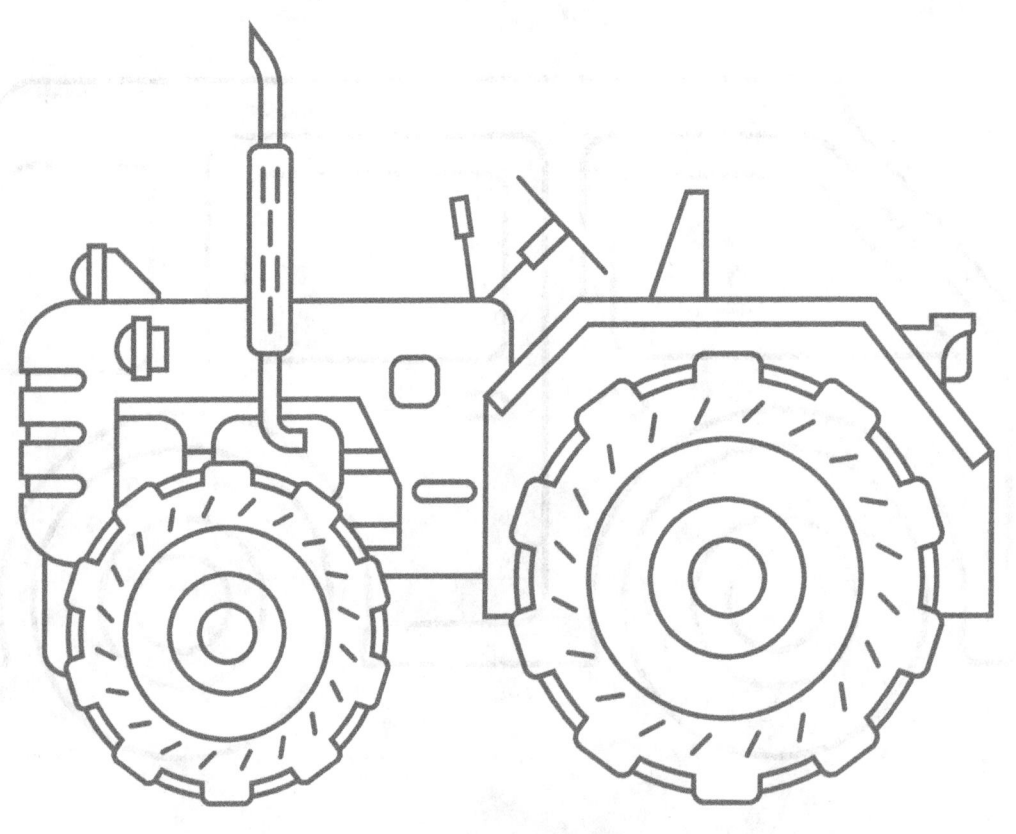

Tractor

Mini Bus

Backhoe Loaders

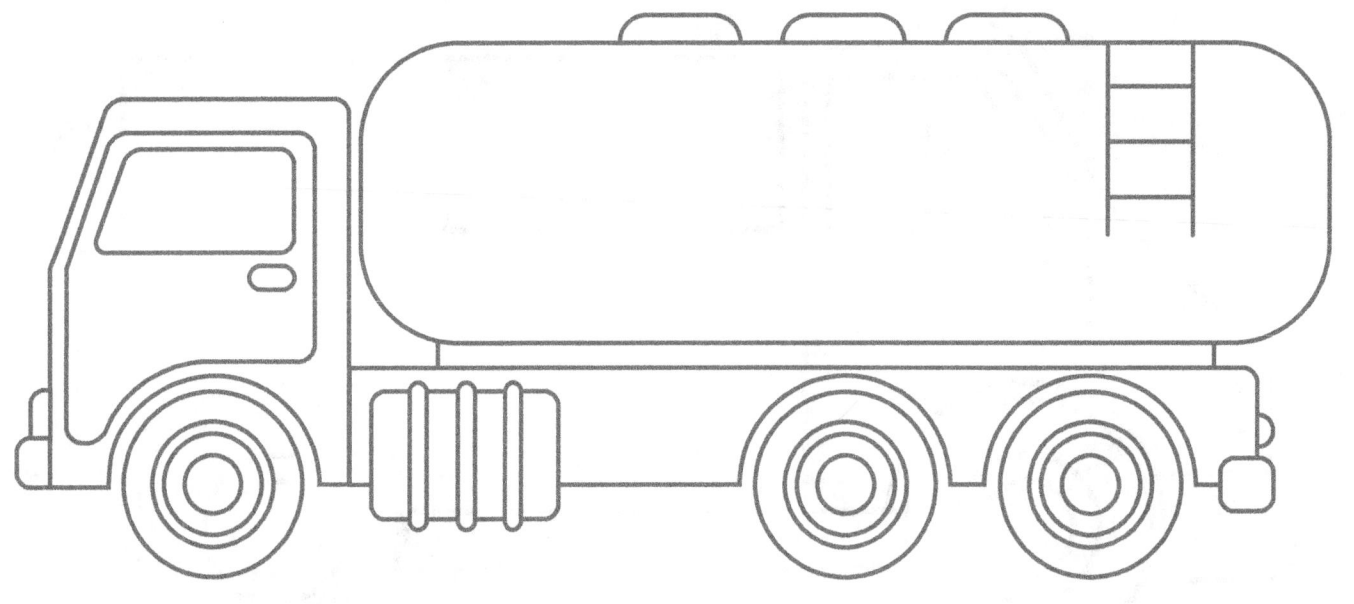

Tanker

Container Truck

Scooter

Cargo Ship

Ambulance

Metro Train

Air Balloon

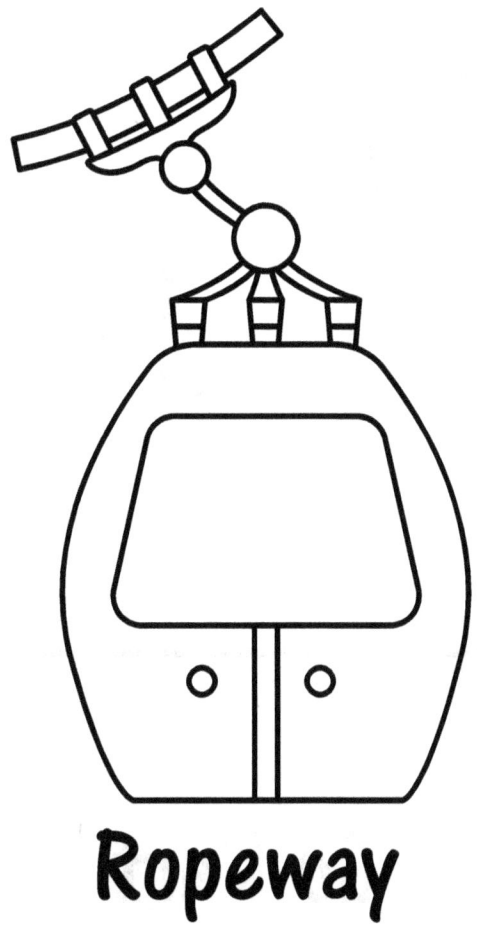

Ropeway

Fire Truck

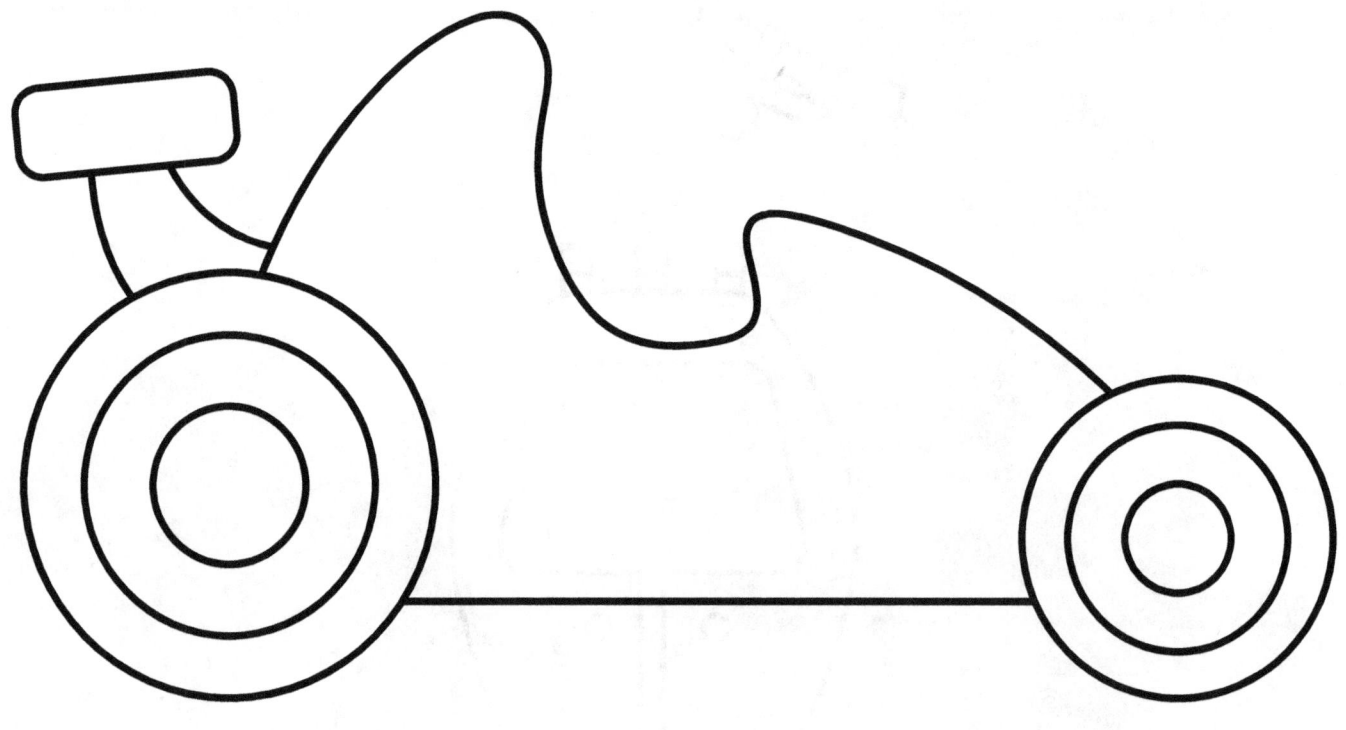

Go Kart

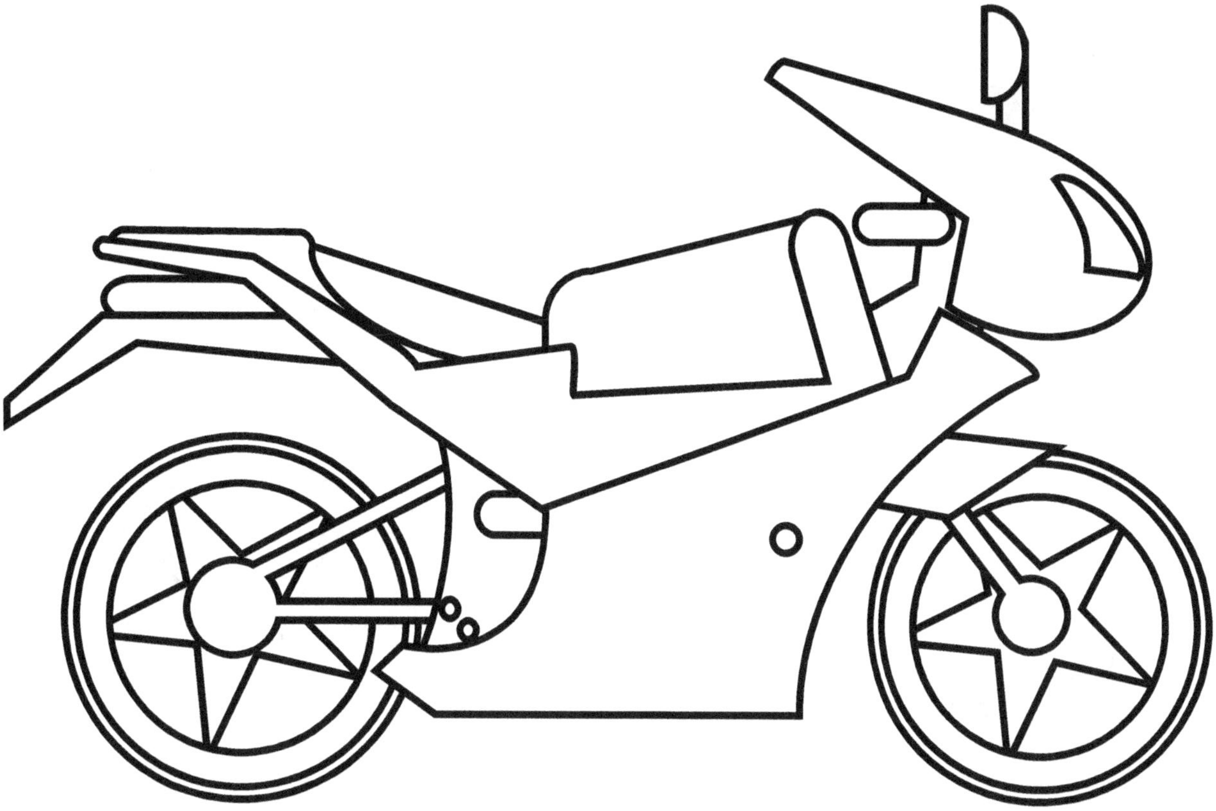

Motorcycle

Taxi / Cab

Electric Scooter

Tow Truck

Castle

Princess

King

Cupcake Cottage

Carriage

Mermaid

Unicorn

Queen

Dragon

Fairy

Prince

Princess on Pony

Crown

Frog

Ship

Pumpkin

Jester Hat

Mermaid

Throne